GEMSTONES OF THE WORLD

DIGGING FOR DIAMONDS

SARAH MACHAJEWSKI

Published in 2018 by The Rosen Publishing Group, Inc.
29 East 21st Street, New York, NY 10010

First Edition

Editor: Theresa Morlock
Book Design: Reann Nye

Photo Credits: Cover roadk/Shutterstock.com; p. 4 Byjeng/Shutterstock.com; p. 5 Maciej Toporowicz, NYC/Moment/Getty Images; p. 6 Africa Studio/Shutterstock.com; p. 7 magnetix/Shutterstock.com; p. 8 Geo-grafika/Shutterstock.com; p. 9 (graphite) Bjoern Wylezich/Shutterstock.com; pp. 9 (diamond), 22 chris kolaczan/Shutterstock.com; p. 10 Manutsawee Buapet/Shutterstock.com; p. 11 Bloomberg/Getty Images; p. 12 Mark S Johnson/Shutterstock.com; p. 13 Rita Saitta/EyeEm/Getty Images; p. 14 Gilles Paire/Shutterstock.com; p. 15 Sementer/Shutterstock.com; p. 16 Great Siberia Studio/Shutterstock.com; p. 17 (polished diamond) pOnGz/Shutterstock.com; p. 17 (raw diamond) Matteo Chinellato/Shutterstock.com; p. 18 The Washington Post/Getty Images; p. 19 The Adventurer/Shutterstock.com; p. 20 resket/Shutterstock.com; p. 21 Paul Velgos/Shutterstock.com.

Cataloging-in-Publication Data

Names: Machajewski, Sarah.
Title: Digging for diamonds / Sarah Machajewski.
Description: New York : PowerKids Press, 2018. | Series: Gemstones of the world | Includes index.
Identifiers: ISBN 9781538328262 (pbk.) | ISBN 9781508164234 (library bound) | ISBN 9781538328323 (6 pack)
Subjects: LCSH: Diamonds–Juvenile literature.
Classification: LCC QE393.M33 2018 | DDC 553.8'2–dc23

Manufactured in the United States of America

CPSIA Compliance Information: Batch Batch #BW18PK: For Further Information contact Rosen Publishing, New York, New York at 1-800-237-9932

CONTENTS

DAZZLING DIAMONDS

Sparkly. Brilliant. Dazzling. These are just some words commonly used to describe diamonds. One of the most popular and sought-after gemstones in the world, diamonds have captured our attention since ancient times. Diamonds are used in some of the most expensive **jewelry** ever created. They're also used in some of our hardest tools, such as blades for cutting.

For as valuable and popular as they are, diamonds are pretty simple gemstones. However, finding them isn't easy. Let's dig into the story of diamonds!

HIDDEN GEMS

Gemstones are usually cut and polished to be used in jewelry.

It's pretty clear why diamonds are so popular. They're beautiful!

WHAT IS A MINERAL?

Diamonds are a kind of mineral. There are thousands of minerals on Earth. To be considered a mineral, a **substance** has to have certain **characteristics**.

Minerals are solids that occur naturally inside Earth. The atoms that make up a mineral determine its characteristics. Atoms are the basic **units** that make up all matter. To form a mineral, atoms must be arranged in a certain way. This arrangement of atoms is called crystal structure.

HIDDEN GEMS

Believe it or not, ice is a mineral—and it's the most common one on Earth's surface!

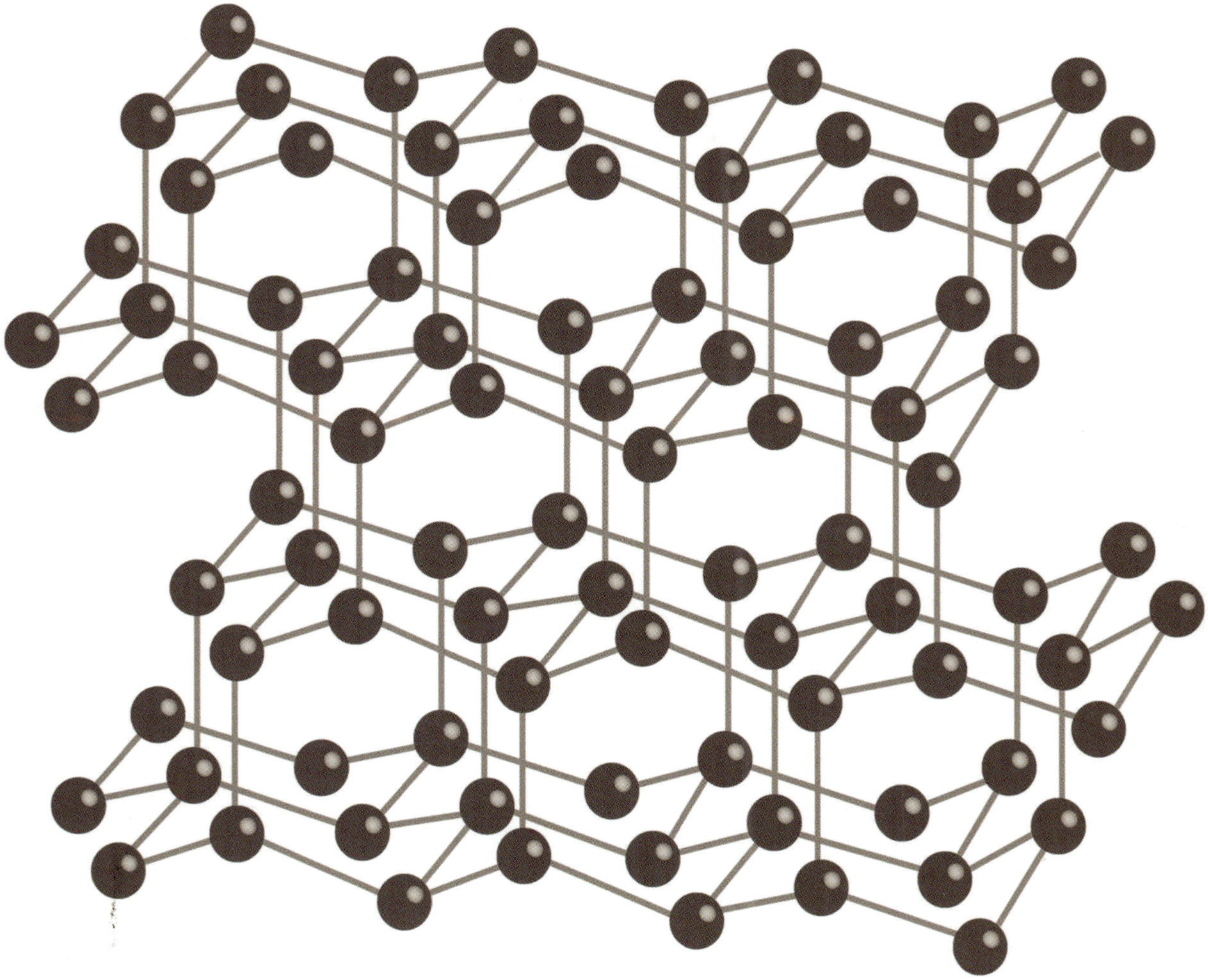

This is a drawing of a diamond's crystal structure. Each atom in a diamond shares a bond with four other atoms. This makes diamonds very strong.

CRAZY CARBON COMBINATIONS

Diamonds are made of pure carbon. Carbon is an element that's found all over the world—in the ground, in coal, and even in the human body! Yet diamonds don't look anything like these things. That's because their atoms are arranged differently.

Graphite and diamond are both minerals made of carbon, but they look very different. Graphite's crystal structure is different from diamond's. The atoms form fewer bonds between each other and are less tightly organized. Graphite isn't nearly as strong as diamond.

COAL

DIAMOND

Diamonds and graphite are two minerals that are made of the same thing but have completely different properties. It all depends on what the mineral's crystal structure is.

GRAPHITE

HOW DIAMONDS FORM

Diamonds form inside the earth at depths of around 100 miles (161 km) or more. They form in the upper mantle, which is one of Earth's four layers. This region has both the heat and pressure needed for diamonds to form.

How hot does it need to be to make diamonds? They form in areas where the temperature is more than 1,832° Fahrenheit (1,000° Celsius). With the weight of the rock layer above, you have the perfect conditions for growing diamonds.

Diamonds can also be created in laboratories by recreating the conditions that cause them to from in nature. These diamonds are called synthetic, or artificial, diamonds. In this photo, a worker in a lab holds up a model of a diamond's structure.

ANCIENT GEMS

Diamonds are old—really old. Scientists believe most diamonds probably formed in the earliest part of the planet's history. Long ago, Earth may have been a hotter planet than it is now. Since diamonds need **extreme** heat to form, the planet's conditions back then were good for growing diamonds.

Most diamonds are probably between 1 billion and 3.5 billion years old. Scientists can't test actual diamonds to learn their age. Instead, they test the age of tiny bits of other minerals found in and near diamonds.

HIDDEN GEMS

The world's oldest diamonds are 4.25 billion years old!

Looking at a diamond under a **microscope** allows you to see its markings, which are called inclusions. Inclusions are like a diamond's birthmarks. They're created during the diamond's formation.

SURFACING

Diamonds form too deep inside Earth for us to ever get to them. So how do they get to us? Long ago, forceful **volcanic eruptions** carried them from the inside of the planet to its surface.

These diamonds were carried in **magma**. As the magma cooled and hardened, diamonds became trapped in the newly formed rock. Kimberlite is the type of **igneous** rock that contains diamonds. As it rose to the surface and cooled, the magma created columns called kimberlite pipes.

HIDDEN GEMS

Diamonds may be found in rivers or in locations where there were once glaciers. They likely end up there as a result of **erosion**.

This yellow diamond is in a piece of kimberlite rock. The diamond is billions of years old, but the rock itself is probably much younger—only about 100 million years old.

DEFINITELY A DIAMOND

People build diamond mines to find the gemstones in kimberlite pipes. Diamonds are pretty rare, or uncommon. Miners have to search through a lot of rocks to find just one. That's why diamonds created in labs are less expensive.

How can you tell if something is a diamond? Diamonds are generally colorless and transparent, which means you can see through them. They're shiny and able to **reflect** light. Finally, diamonds are very, very hard. In fact, they're one of the hardest-known substances on Earth.

DIAMOND MINE, YAKUTSK, RUSSIA

ROUGH DIAMOND

Rough diamonds are diamonds as they're found in nature. Through a process of cutting and polishing, rough diamonds are turned into brilliant gemstones. Then, they're ready to be used in jewelry.

CUT AND POLISHED DIAMOND

A BEAUTIFUL VARIETY

Every diamond is different, which is part of what makes them so wonderful. Diamonds can be colorless, black, or many different kinds of colors. There are blue, yellow, pink, orange, and green diamonds. These diamonds are very rare—and valuable.

Brown and gray diamonds are not as valuable, so they're usually used to make tools. Some diamonds are extremely clear, while others are opaque, which means you can't see through them. It all depends on what the conditions were inside Earth when the diamond formed.

HIDDEN GEMS

The Hope Diamond is a large, blue-violet stone that was found long ago in a mine in India. It has been owned by a king of France and by a number of very rich people. Today, the 45.52-carat stone belongs to the Smithsonian Institution in Washington, D.C.

A carat is the unit for measuring the weight of jewels such as diamonds. One carat is equal to 0.007 ounce (0.2 g).

THE HUMAN SIDE OF DIAMONDS

Diamonds are highly sought after. Centuries ago, diamonds were only owned by very rich people because they were so hard to find. Today, modern diamond mines produce more diamonds than ever before. Diamonds are still rare, though.

The most popular use of diamonds is in jewelry such as rings, earrings, and necklaces. People buy diamonds to give as gifts. Diamonds are also used to make blades for cutting tools. It's the perfect material since diamonds are so hard. Diamond-tipped blades can cut through stone and concrete.

DIAMOND-TIPPED SAW BLADE

Diamonds make for eye-catching jewelry. They can reflect more light than other gemstones, which is why they're so sparkly.

GLOBAL IMPACT

Diamonds can cost a lot of money. The quest for these valuable gemstones can sometimes hurt the people involved. Some diamond mines use practices that are harmful to miners.

Fortunately, these struggles have improved in recent years. We can help by not buying diamonds from mines that don't treat workers fairly.

More and more diamonds are found every day. Whether worn as jewelry or used in other ways, diamonds will probably always be one of the world's most popular gemstones.

GLOSSARY

characteristic: A special quality that makes a person, thing, or group different from others.

erosion: The wearing away of Earth's surface by wind or water.

extreme: Very great in degree.

igneous: A type of rock that's made from hardened lava or magma.

jewelry: Objects people wear on their body for decoration, often made of special metals or prized stones.

magma: Hot, liquid rock below the surface of Earth.

microscope: An instrument used for viewing very small objects.

reflect: To throw back light, heat, or sound without absorbing it, or taking it in.

substance: A particular kind of matter.

unit: A single thing, person, or group that is part of something larger.

volcanic eruption: An event in which a volcano, or an opening in a planet's surface through which hot, liquid rock sometimes flows, sends out that rock and other substances in a sudden explosion.

INDEX

WEBSITES

Due to the changing nature of Internet links, PowerKids Press has developed an online list of websites related to the subject of this book. This site is updated regularly. Please use this link to access the list: www.powerkidslinks.com/gotw/dia